To Inga Terauda

⋟ • ⋞

The Snow Queen

Copyright © 2013 by Bagram Ibatoulline

www.harpercollinschildrens.com

Retelling by Allison Grace MacDonald

Library of Congress Cataloging-in-Publication Data

The Snow Queen : a retelling of the fairy tale / by Hans Christian Andersen ; illustrated by Bagram Ibatoulline. — 1st ed.

    p.   cm.

Summary: The strength of a little girl's love enables her to overcome many obstacles and free a boy from the Snow Queen's spell.

ISBN 978-0-06-220950-4 (hardcover bdg.)

[1. Fairy tales.]   I. Ibatoulline, Bagram, ill.   II. Andersen, H. C. (Hans Christian), 1805–1875. Snedronningen.

PZ7.S41545   2013   2012011533

[E]—dc23   CIP

                                                                  AC

The artist used acryl-gouache paint on paper to create the illustrations for this book.

Typography by Martha Rago

13 14 15 16 17 SCP 10 9 8 7 6 5 4 3 2 1

❖

First Edition

The Snow Queen

A RETELLING OF THE FAIRY TALE BY

Hans Christian Andersen

ILLUSTRATED BY

Bagram Ibatoulline

HARPER

An Imprint of HarperCollinsPublishers

ONCE UPON A TIME, *a wicked troll created a powerful*

mirror. Everything good that was reflected in the mirror looked ugly and horrible.
Everything evil looked appealing.

The troll was proud of his creation. He decided to bring the mirror up into the heavens
to make fun of the angels there. Higher and higher he flew, laughing along the way. The
higher he flew, the more he laughed, until he could barely hold on to the mirror. The mirror slipped
out of his hands and fell to the ground, where it broke into millions of pieces.

The pieces, as small as tiny grains of sand, were picked up and carried by the wind across the earth.
If a flake like that got into someone's eye, that person would forever see everything distorted. If a
splinter got into someone's heart, that heart would turn to ice.

The troll laughed even harder about this. He couldn't wait to see the evil his mirror would inflict
upon the world.

$\mathcal{I}$N AN OLD CITY, there lived two families who shared a small rose garden between their houses. A girl named Gerda lived in one house with her grandmother, and a boy named Kai lived in the other. They were best friends, as close as brother and sister. In the summer, they would open their windows, step outside, and be together. In the winter, they would defrost their windows and wave at each other across the garden.

One winter day, Grandma, Kai, and Gerda watched the snow fall outside the window.

"Look at those white bees swarm," Grandma said.

"Do snowflakes have a queen like bees do?" Kai asked.

"Yes, they do," Grandma said. "The Snow Queen flies at the center of a snowstorm. She blows onto windows and makes ice flowers."

Gerda imagined the Snow Queen and shivered. "Could she come indoors if you left the window open?"

"If she comes inside, I will melt her with the warmth from the stove and turn her into a puddle at my feet," Kai said boldly.

Just then a gust of icy-cold wind opened the window and threw a whirl of snow into the room. Kai ran to the window to shut it. "Ouch!" he cried from pain when something stung his eye.

It was a small piece of the evil mirror that had flown in with the snow. The next moment, another splinter got into Kai's heart. And right away his world changed—everything beautiful started to look ugly to him, and everything bad was pleasing.

"What happened? Did the snow get into your eyes?" asked Gerda, looking worried.

"Get off me, girl! I am sick and tired of sitting here and listening to stupid stories! I am going outside to ride my sled."

"But it is so late!" Gerda was surprised by Kai's sudden change.

"I don't care! I do what I want," said Kai as he put on his coat.

Gerda began to cry.

"You look ugly when you cry," Kai said, before stomping away and leaving Gerda.

Kai ran outside to join the older children sledding in the snow until out of the darkness came a large, ornate sleigh into the town square. It drove so fast that Kai didn't even have time to take a closer look at it, but he managed to tie his sled behind this fine sleigh. The sleigh sped up, pulling Kai from the town square and through the city gates, farther than Kai had ever been before. Snowfall turned into blizzard, and Kai couldn't see anything around him. He was very cold and very scared. The other town children headed home, but Kai stubbornly clung to his sled.

The snow fell harder, and the snowflakes grew bigger. Finally, the sleigh came to a silent stop. The driver turned to look at Kai, her eyes piercing the storm.

It was the Snow Queen!

"Come, Kai. Come sit with me and get warm." The Snow Queen's voice whistled like the winter wind.

Kai climbed into the sleigh and pulled a fur blanket over himself. The Snow Queen kissed him once on the forehead, and he was warm. She kissed him again, and he couldn't remember anything: not Gerda, not Grandma, and not his house with the tiny garden.

He stared up at the moon all night long as the snowstorm whipped around him. When day broke, he slept at the feet of the Snow Queen.

As time passed, no one knew where Kai had gone. Most believed he had drowned in the icy river, but not Gerda. She often looked out her window at the empty garden and wished that Kai would come home.

Winter turned into spring, and Gerda went to the river with her new red shoes and dropped them into the water.

"I will give you my new shoes if you will give me back my friend," she told the river.

The current carried her shoes right back to her. The river didn't want her shoes, because the river hadn't taken Kai. But Gerda thought she just needed to get farther from shore before offering her shoes. She stepped into a little boat and untied it from the dock. Too late she realized she hadn't any oars to control the boat. The current carried it along with helpless Gerda inside.

All the way downriver, Gerda finally reached land. She climbed out of the boat and cried for help. Her calls were answered by an old woman, who helped her to her feet and welcomed her into her home.

The old woman was lonely and wanted Gerda to stay forever. After listening to Gerda's story, she snuck outside into the garden and used magic to remove all her roses. She did not want anything to remind Gerda of home.

Gerda decided to stay and rest awhile. She almost forgot about her journey to find Kai, until one day many months later when the old woman put on a large-brimmed hat that was decorated with roses. Gerda again remembered her friend. She went out into the garden, determined to find out from the flowers what had happened to Kai.

One by one Gerda asked the tiger lilies, the honeysuckles, the daisies, and the buttercups. Each told her a story about someone lost, but they didn't know about Kai.

Gerda knelt in the dirt and wept.

As her tears splashed onto the ground and mixed into the soil, the roses reappeared.

"We have been down under the earth," they said. "We know that Kai is not dead."

Gerda knew then that she had to keep looking. She had to find Kai and bring him home, so she continued her journey.

Gerda kept walking. Every day the air grew colder and colder and Gerda became more tired. When the first snow of winter had fallen to the ground, Gerda was approached by a crow. Gerda was lonely, and she told the crow her story and asked if he had seen Kai.

"Maybe, maybe," the crow said. "The boy I've seen now lives with a princess."

The land they were on belonged to a princess who not long ago had decided to get married. She had decreed that all the eligible men in the land could come to the castle and woo her. Whoever was most clever would receive the princess's hand in marriage.

The crow had watched the eager men line up at the palace. There he saw a boy with eyes like Gerda's and brown hair.

"That must be Kai!" Gerda said.

"He was carrying a knapsack."

"You must mean his sled," Gerda corrected.

"This boy was so clever that the princess chose him to be her husband."

"Surely that's Kai," Gerda said. "Can you take me to him?"

Gerda followed the crow through the royal garden and to a short door in the back of the castle. The door opened onto a dark, winding staircase. Once up the stairs, they passed from one ornate hallway to the next before arriving at the royal bedchamber.

Gerda pushed the door open and peered at the sleeping bodies. The prince had his back to her, and she could only hear him breathing. He had a head of brown hair. It was Kai!

Gerda raced to his side and shook him awake. The prince and princess awoke and lit the lamp between their beds.

By the glow of the light, Gerda saw the prince's face. It wasn't Kai after all. She couldn't help but weep. She had been so sure that her journey had ended and that she and Kai would be reunited.

The prince and princess listened to Gerda's story. They were good people, and they wanted to help the poor girl.

The next morning, they dressed Gerda in the finest clothes of silk and velvet.

"You are welcome to stay with us," the princess said. But Gerda knew she couldn't. Kai was still out there, and she needed to find him.

The prince and princess outfitted her with warm boots and a muff and gave her a golden coach with her own driver and horse.

"Good-bye and good luck!" they said to her, and waved as her carriage pulled away.

Gerda was very warm, and glad to be moving much faster than on foot. But her comfort didn't last long. In the dark forest, her golden carriage shone like the moon.

"Gold!" voices cried, and the carriage came to a sudden halt. Robbers attacked them. They stole her horse and killed the driver, then dragged Gerda out of the coach and onto the ground.

"Let's kill her too!" someone cried, and Gerda covered her face in fear.

"Stop!" a small voice piped up. "Don't kill her. She could come home with me and be my playmate." The voice belonged to a robber girl who was very spoiled and always got what she wanted.

"I won't let them kill you, but you must not make me angry. Do you promise?" the robber girl asked.

The robber girl took Gerda home with her. She boasted about her collection of animals, all stolen.

"And those are my doves," the robber girl said, pointing to the birds perched on the rafters. "I keep them locked inside because otherwise they will fly off."

Gerda was quite frightened and she started to cry. She told the robber girl her whole story and how much she missed Kai.

"Come and sleep over here. I can protect you." The robber girl showed Gerda where to sleep, then curled up nearby, tucking a knife under her pillow. That night as the robber girl slept, the doves spoke to Gerda.

"We have seen Kai," they said. "He rode in the Snow Queen's sleigh. They were going to Lapland, where it is always winter."

"How do I get there?" Gerda asked.

"Ask the reindeer," the birds said. "He is from Lapland."

In the morning when Gerda told the robber girl about what the doves had said, the girl decided to help Gerda escape. She snuck her past the rest of her family and gave her the reindeer.

"Take this girl with you to Lapland," she instructed the reindeer. "By doing this, you have earned your freedom from me."

The reindeer was overjoyed. He allowed Gerda to climb onto his back, and they took off into the wilderness. They journeyed day after day with little rest, traveling farther and farther north.

"Look at the northern lights," said the reindeer. The colors danced across the dark sky, and the reindeer and the girl pushed onward.

Finally, the pair arrived in Lapland. They stopped at the first house they saw, eager to get out of the cold.

The Lapp woman welcomed them and said, "You still have a hundred miles to go. From here you can see the fireworks that the Snow Queen shoots into the sky every night to entertain herself." The Lapp woman instructed them to find the Finnish woman who lives near the Snow Queen's palace.

When they reached the Finnish woman's home, the fire was so strong and the house was so warm that Gerda took off her boots and mittens. The Finnish woman gave the reindeer ice to cool him down and whispered to him that Kai was living in the Snow Queen's palace.

"He thinks it's the best place in the world. He has a sliver of glass in his heart and a grain of glass in his eye. This keeps the Snow Queen's power over him."

"Can't you help the poor girl?" the reindeer begged. "Can you give her power to remove the glass?"

"Don't you see she has the power within her?" the Finnish woman said. "Look at all the animals and people who have served her. Look how far she has come, when she started out with nothing but bare feet. That is her true power. Take her to the Snow Queen's garden and then come back. She will be able to save Kai on her own."

The Finnish woman put Gerda on the reindeer's back and sent them off.

"I don't have my mittens or boots," Gerda said. But the reindeer kept running. He stopped at the Snow Queen's garden, let Gerda climb off, and then ran away before Gerda could protest.

Gerda stood alone at the gates to the Snow Queen's garden. The snow stung her feet and the wind whistled in her ears. With the palace in sight, she ran through the garden as quickly as her numb feet would carry her. The snow darted in every direction, and as she drew closer, the snowflakes grew bigger. They took the form of spears aimed directly at little Gerda.

Gerda continued on, thinking only of her lost friend.

Meanwhile, at the Snow Queen's palace, Kai was there alone.

"I'm going to the warm countries with the volcanoes," the Snow Queen had said that morning. "I thought I could chalk their peaks a bit." The Snow Queen flew away, and Kai sat by himself on the icy palace floor.

The palace walls were made of snow. The windows were made of wind and ice. The hallways were several miles long and were lit only by the northern lights.

In the middle of the palace there was a frozen lake. In the middle of the lake was the Snow Queen's throne. The lake itself was cracked into millions of pieces of ice. The Snow Queen had told Kai that if he could form the word "eternity" with the pieces, he would be free.

That was how Gerda found Kai. He was sitting on the icy floor in the empty hall, black and blue from the cold, arranging and rearranging the pieces of ice.

"Kai!" Gerda cried. "At last I have found you."

Gerda ran to him and held him in her arms. His body was stiff and cold, and his eyes looked up at her without recognition.

"Kai, sweet Kai, come back to me," Gerda begged. She cried as she held him, and her tears fell onto his chest deep into his heart and melted the ice. He looked up at Gerda and wept. His own tears cleared his sight once again.

"Gerda!" Kai said. "My dear friend. Where have you been? What happened to me?"

Gerda told him every part of her journey, from her red shoes in the river to the roses in the old woman's garden, the crow, the prince and princess, the robber girl, and the reindeer who had brought her here. She kissed his cheeks and his cold fingers and watched his color return.

Kai and Gerda were so happy that they stood up and danced. They danced on the icy lake, and the ice danced with them. When the ice stopped, it lay down and formed the word "eternity." Now even if the Snow Queen were to return, Kai had earned his freedom.

Hand in hand, Gerda and Kai walked out of the palace. The reindeer was waiting for them in the garden to take them to the border of Lapland.

Soon the snow began to melt. Spring was here. Gerda and Kai traveled together through the forest.

At the edge of the forest, they came upon the river, and in the distance was their city. They followed the river upstream, and soon they were back on their old street.

They walked up the steps to see Grandma. Everything inside looked the same. The same furniture and the same tick-tock of the clock. But as they stepped through the doorway, they realized that they had changed: They were no longer children.

The two friends sat on their old chairs and held hands. As they looked at the roses in the garden, all memory of the Snow Queen disappeared.

There they sat as grown-ups, but in their hearts they were still children. Outside, it was sunny and warm. A perfect summer day.